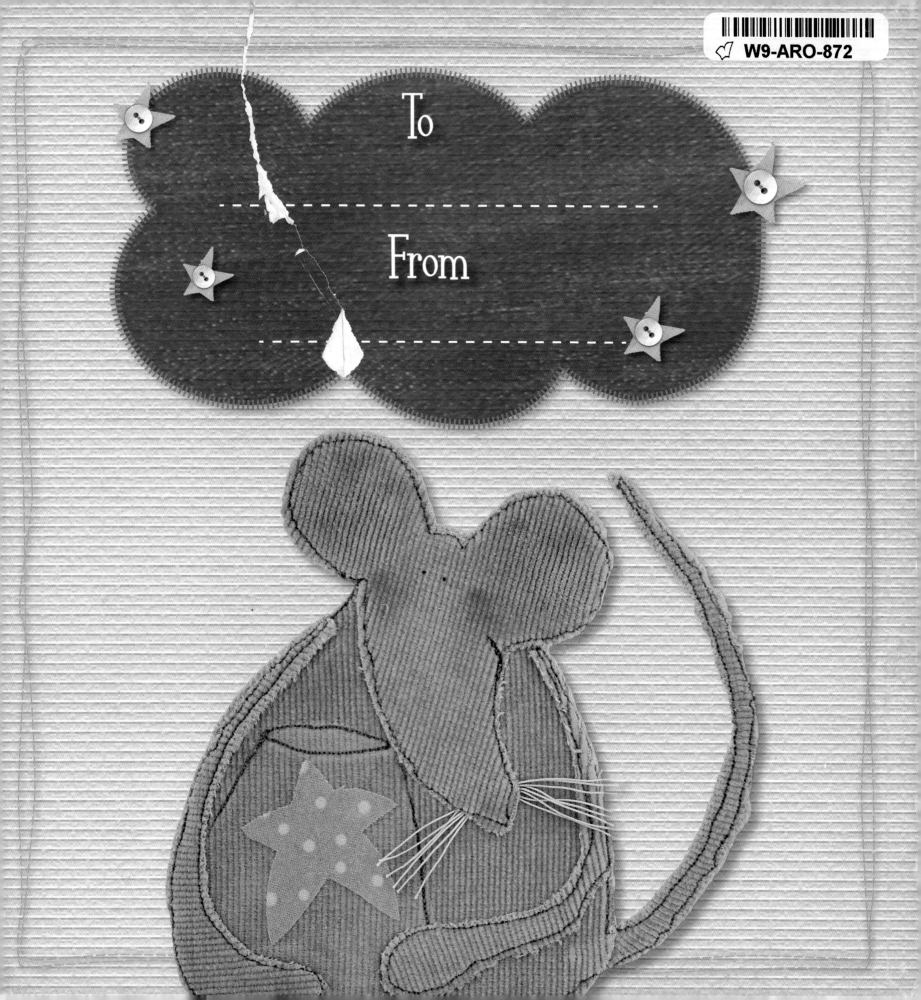

To

From

With thanks to Jane Horne.

Copyright © 2007

make believe ideas

27 Castle Street, Berkhamsted,
Hertfordshire, HP4 2DW.

Manufactured in China

# TWINKLE TWINKLE
## LiTTLE STAR

KATE TOMS

make
believe
ideas

Twinkle, twinkle,
little star,
How I wonder
what you are,

You **shine** above
the **world** so high,
Like a **lightbulb**
in the **sky**.

I'd love to catch you in my net...

and keep you as a special pet!

Twinkle, twinkle, little **star**,
I do so **wonder** what **you** are.

When snuggled up in bed at night,

Cozy, warm, and tucked up tight,

I dream that I can fly a rocket...

5 4 3 2

and gather stardust in my pocket.

Twinkle, twinkle,

little **star**,

How I wonder

what **you** are.

Does a **man** live on the **moon?**

And if the **moon**

Yummy!

is made of **cheese,**

Will you save some for me, please?

Twinkle, twinkle, little star,
What do you see from afar?

Hello

Hola!

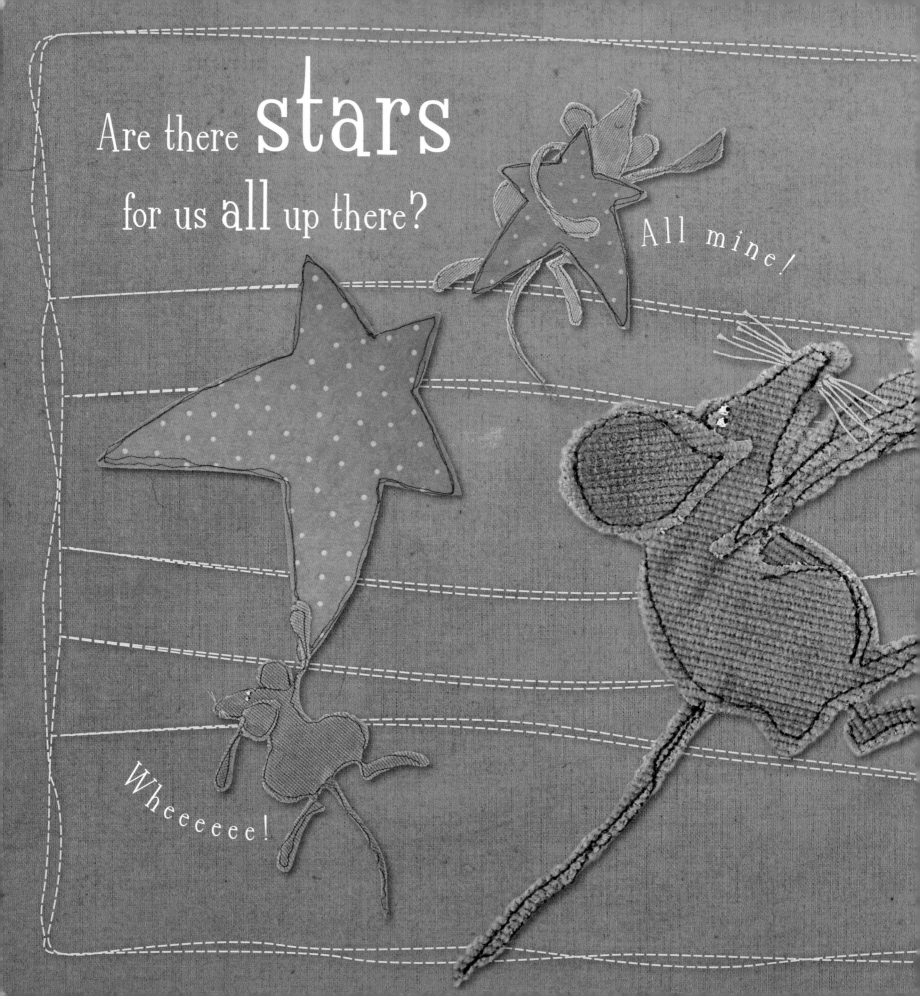

Are there **stars** for us **all** up there?

All mine!

Wheeeeee!

Jump!

Or do some folks have to share?

Twinkle, twinkle, little **star**, How I wonder what **you** are!

When the **sky** grows **dark** at **night**, I **wish** and **wish** with all my **might**,

That you would look down on my **house**, And grant one thing for this small **mouse**.

And see the world the way you do.

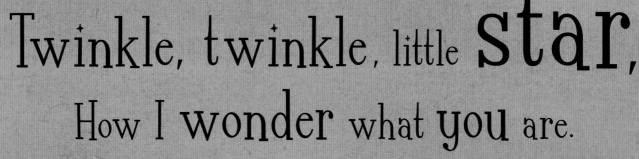

Twinkle, twinkle, little star,
How I wonder what you are.

When it's time to climb the stairs,

To brush my teeth and say my prayers,

Through my window I can see,
That you are smiling down on me.

Twinkle, twinkle, little **star**, How I wonder what **you** are,

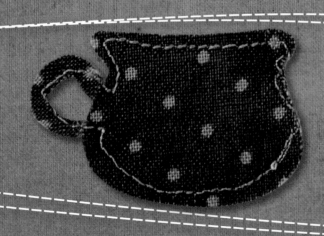